Milwaukee BUCKS

BY JIM GIGLIOTTI

Published by The Child's World®
1980 Lookout Drive • Mankato, MN 56003-1705
800-599-READ • www.childsworld.com

Cover: © Darren Abate/AP Images.
Photographs ©: AP Images: Morry Gash 6, 13; Ozier Muhammad/Ebony Collection 17; Paul Shane 22; Todd Warshaw/Icon SW 29. Imagn/USA Today Sports: Benny Sieu 5, 10; Jeff Hanisch 26; John Sokolowski 26. Newscom: Curtis Compton/TNS 9; Stephen Dowell/MCT 18; Icon SW 25; Adam Davis/Icon SW 26; Joe Robbins: 21, 26.

Copyright © 2020 by The Child's World®
All rights reserved. No part of this book may be reproduced or utilized in any form or by any means without written permission from the publisher.

ISBN 9781503824546
LCCN 2018964288

Printed in the United States of America
PA02416

ABOUT THE AUTHOR

Jim Gigliotti has worked for the University of Southern California, the Los Angeles Dodgers, and the National Football League. He is now an author who has written more than 100 books, mostly for young readers, on a variety of topics.

TABLE OF CONTENTS

Go, Bucks! 4
Who Are the Bucks? 7
Where They Came From. 8
Who They Play 11
Where They Play 12
The Basketball Court 15
Good Times. 16
Tough Times 19
All the Right Moves 20
Heroes Then 23
Heroes Now 24
What They Wear 27

    Team Stats 28
    Glossary 30
    Find Out More 31
    Index 32

GO, BUCKS!

The Bucks have had many highs and many lows. The high was as high as it gets. The team won the NBA title in 1971. That came after an amazing rise. It was only the team's third season. The Bucks have not won another title since. There have been many good years, however. That includes the 2018-19 season. The Bucks just missed the NBA Finals! They look like a team on the rise again.

Milwaukee's Giannis Antetokounmpo grew up in Greece. He has become one of the NBA's most exciting players.

5

Brook Lopez is seven feet (2.1 m) tall. That height helps him reach above opponents to make baskets.

6

WHO ARE THE BUCKS?

The Bucks play in the NBA Central Division. That division is part of the Eastern Conference. The other teams in the Central Division are the Chicago Bulls, the Cleveland Cavaliers, the Detroit Pistons, and the Indiana Pacers. The Bucks have finished in first place 13 times in their history. They have won the conference title twice.

WHERE THEY CAME FROM

The Bucks were an NBA **expansion team** in the 1969 season. The team held a contest for its name. The most popular name was Robins. A robin is a small bird. The second choice was Bucks. A buck is a male animal, especially a deer. The winning entry said that bucks "are good jumpers, fast, and **agile**." Good basketball players are those things, too! The team chose to be the Bucks.

Giannis Antetokounmpo gets the ball upcourt. His uniform shows one of the Bucks large deer head logos.

Milwaukee's Pat Connaughton stands tough against a Western Conference opponent, the Golden State Warriors.

WHO THEY PLAY

The Bucks play 82 games each season. They play 41 games at home and 41 on the road. They play four games against each of the other Central Division teams. They play 36 games against other Eastern Conference teams. Finally, the Bucks play each of the teams in the Western Conference twice. That's a lot of basketball! Each June, the winners of the Western and Eastern Conferences play each other in the NBA Finals.

WHERE THEY PLAY

The Bucks moved into a brand-new arena in the 2019 season. It is the Fiserv Forum. Many Bucks fans call it the "Four-One-Forum." That is because the city's telephone area code is 414. A **mascot** named Bango entertains the fans. Why Bango? It was a made-up word by one of the team's announcers. He used it when the team made a long shot.

Say hello to Bango the Buck, the Milwaukee team mascot. He helps fans cheer at the Bucks' home court.

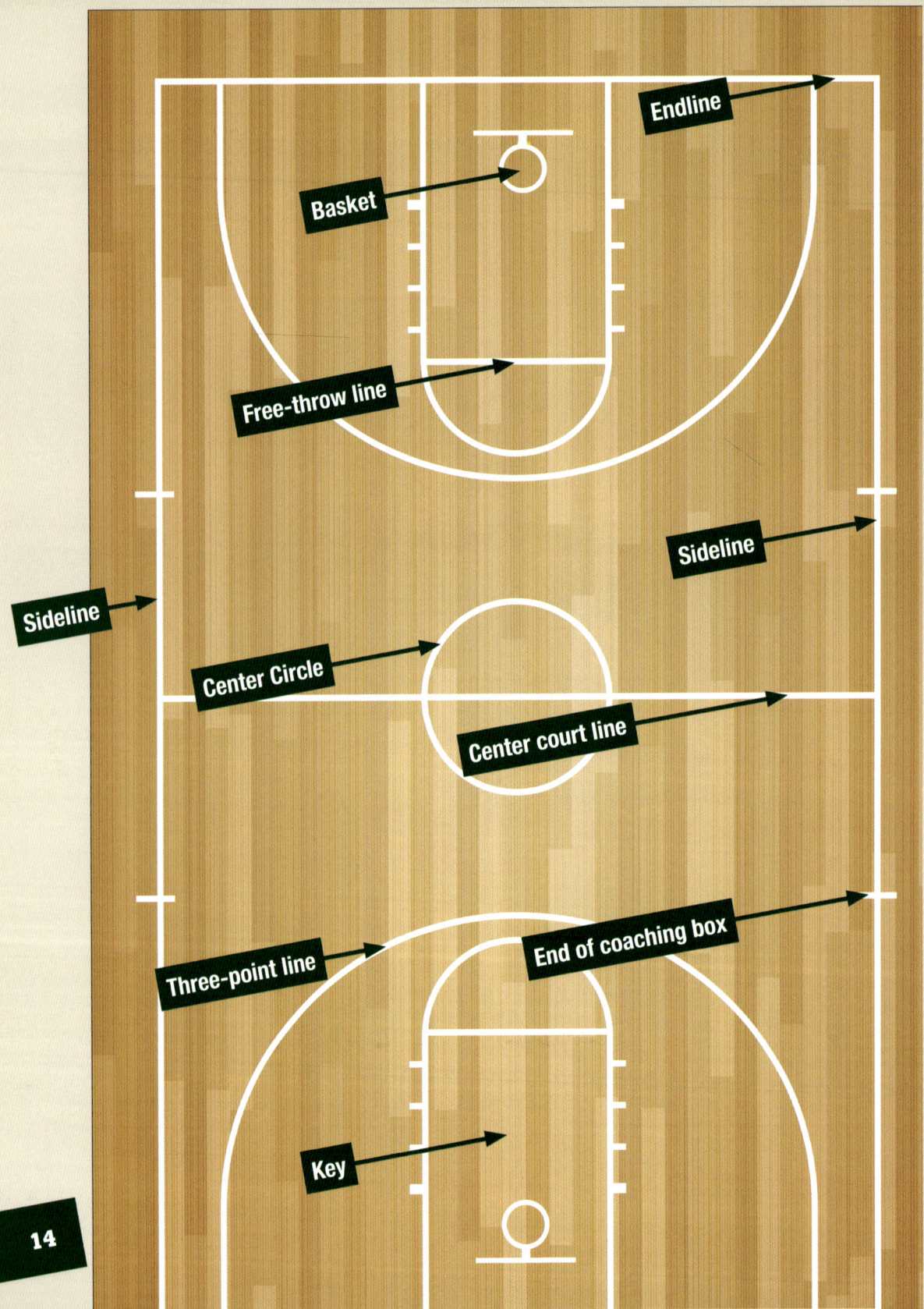

THE BASKETBALL COURT

An NBA court is 94 feet long and 50 feet wide (28.6 m by 15.24 m). Nearly all the courts are made from hard maple wood. Rubber mats under the wood help make the floor springy. Each team paints the court with its **logo** and colors. Lines on the court show the players where to take shots. The diagram on the left shows the important parts of the NBA court.

The video displays on the scoreboard at the Fiserv Forum are the largest in the NBA.

GOOD TIMES

The Bucks won a coin toss after their first season to pick first in the **draft**. They chose **center** Lew Alcindor. He changed his name to Kareem Abdul-Jabbar. He led the team to the NBA title in 1971. In 1972, the Bucks beat the Lakers 120–104. The Bucks' win ended the Lakers' record 33-game winning streak. In 2019, the Bucks reached the Western Conference finals.

Kareem Abdul-Jabbar began his Hall of Fame career in Milwaukee.

17

The Orlando Magic stuffed this basket against the Bucks in 2014 as Milwaukee struggled all season.

TOUGH TIMES

In June 1975, the Bucks traded star center Kareem Abdul-Jabbar. The team won only 38 games that season. It won only 30 games the next. Bucks fans would like to forget a game against the Jazz in 1990. Utah's Karl Malone scored 61 points. The Bucks lost by 48. The team missed the playoffs seven years in a row in the 1990s. In 2014, the Bucks won only 15 games. It was their lowest total ever.

ALL THE RIGHT MOVES

Kareem Abdul-Jabbar shot his "sky hook" from way above his head. It was impossible to stop. Current star Giannis Antetokounmpo's best moves are with his feet. He is great at the "Euro step." He stops his dribble. Then he quickly changes direction to go around a defender. It takes great balance. Antetokounmpo often finishes the play with a layup or a dunk.

In basketball, a "big man" means a player who is tall and strong. It can also refer to a team's best player.

After faking to his right, Giannis Antetokounmpo dribbles to the left, showing off his Euro step move.

21

The Big O, Oscar Robertson, thrilled Milwaukee with some of the best all-around skills in the game.

HEROES THEN

Kareem Abdul-Jabbar scored more points than anyone else in league history. He had more rebounds than anyone else in team history. **Guard** Oscar Roberston was one of the best all-around players ever. "The Big O" was a great scorer, passer, and defender. **Forward** Glenn Robinson regularly averaged more than 20 points per game. Guard Michael Redd did, too.

HEROES NOW

Giannis Antetokounmpo is a superstar. He has the power of a big man. He has the moves of a smaller player. He was an all-star for the second year in a row in 2018. Khris Middleton and Malcolm Brogdon helped give the Bucks a great offense in 2019. Middleton passes the ball as well as he shoots it. Brogdon became a full-time starter in 2019.

Young Malcolm Brogdon launches a shot against the Wizards.

Bucks Uniforms

WHAT THEY WEAR

NBA players wear a **tank top** jersey. Players wear team shorts. Each player can choose his own sneakers. Some players also wear knee pads or wrist guards.

Each NBA team has more than one jersey style. The pictures at left show some of the Bucks' jerseys.

The NBA basketball is 29.5 inches (75 cm) around. It is covered with leather. The leather has small bumps called pebbles.

The pebbles on a basketball help players grip it.

TEAM STATS

Here are some of the all-time career records for the Milwaukee Bucks. These stats are complete through all of the 2018–19 NBA regular season.

GAMES
Junior Bridgeman	711
Sidney Moncrief	695

POINTS PER GAME
Kareem Abdul-Jabbar	30.4
Glenn Robinson	21.1

ASSISTS PER GAME
Oscar Robertson	7.5
Sam Cassell	7.2

REBOUNDS PER GAME
Kareem Abdul-Jabbar	15.3
Elmore Smith	9.8

STEALS PER GAME
Alvin Robertson	2.7
Quinn Buckner	2.3

FREE-THROW PCT.
Malcolm Brogdon	.895
Jack Sikma	.884

RAY ALLEN

THREE-POINT FIELD GOALS

Ray Allen	1,051
Michael Redd	1,003

29

GLOSSARY

agile *(ADJ-uhl)* the ability to move quickly and easily

center *(SEN-ter)* a basketball position that plays near the basket

draft *(DRAFT)* an event at which NBA teams choose new players

expansion team *(ex-PAN-shun TEEM)* in sports, a team that is added to an existing league

forward *(FORE-word)* a player who usually plays away from the basket

guard *(GARD)* a player who usually dribbles and makes passes

logo *(LOW-go)* a team or company's symbol

mascot *(MASS-kot)* a costumed character who helps fans cheer

tank top *(TANK TOP)* a style of shirt that has straps over the shoulders and no sleeves

FIND OUT MORE

IN THE LIBRARY

Bryant, Howard. *Legends: The Best Players, Games, and Teams in Basketball.* New York, NY: Philomel Books, 2016.

Goodman, Michael E. *Milwaukee Bucks.* Mankato, MN: Creative Paperbacks, 2018.

Schaller, Bob with Coach Dave Harnish. *The Everything Kids' Basketball Book.* Avon, MA: Adams Media, 2017.

ON THE WEB

Visit our website for links about the Milwaukee Bucks:
childsworld.com/links

Note to Parents, Teachers, and Librarians: We routinely verify our Web links to make sure they are safe and active sites. So encourage your readers to check them out!

INDEX

Abdul-Jabbar, Kareem, 16, 17, 19, 20, 23
Alcindor, Lew, 16
Antetokounmpo, Giannis, 5, 9, 20, 21, 24
Bango, 12, 13
Brogdon, Malcolm, 24, 25
Central Division, 7, 11
Chicago Bulls, 7
Cleveland Cavaliers, 7
Connaughton, Pat, 10
court, 9, 13, 15
Detroit Pistons, 7
Eastern Conference, 7, 11
Fiserv Forum, 12, 15
Golden State Warriors, 10
Indiana Pacers, 7
jerseys, 27
Lopez, Brook, 6
Los Angeles Lakers, 16
Malone, Karl, 19
Middleton, Khris, 24
Orlando Magic, 18
Redd, Michael, 23
Robertson, Oscar, 22, 23
Robins, 8
Robinson, Glenn, 23
Utah Jazz, 19
Western Conference, 10, 11